CYNDY SZEKERES'
Book

of Fairy Tales

Adapted and illustrated
by Cyndy Szekeres

A GOLDEN BOOK • NEW YORK
Western Publishing Company, Inc.,
Racine, Wisconsin 53404

Table of Contents

The Brementown Musicians

There was once a donkey who lived on a farm. He earned his oats and hay by carting sacks of wheat from the fields to the mill, where it was ground into flour. When the donkey grew too old and weary for such a task, he decided to leave the farm and go to live in the nearby town of Bremen. He thought he might become a street musician there. He could entertain the townspeople with old songs he had learned and use the coins they would toss him for food and lodging.

He had not traveled far when he saw a dog lying near the road. "How now, friend?" said the donkey.

"I've been running away," said the dog. "I have grown too old to hunt, and I wish to try something new."

"Why not come with me?" asked the donkey. "I am going to try my luck as a musician in Bremen. Dogs have powerful voices, so perhaps you could do the same."

The dog liked the idea. "But I'm too tired to walk all the way to Bremen," he said with a sigh.

"Hop up onto my back, and we can practice our singing as we go along," said the donkey.

Each time the donkey said, "Hee, haw! Hee, hee, haw!" the dog would bark, "Bow, woof, bow, wow!"

Not long after, they met a sad and sorry cat. The frown on her face was as long as a lonesome road in winter.

"What is the matter?" asked the donkey.

"I am getting old," said the cat, "and I cannot catch mice anymore. I ran away to try something new, but I don't know which way to go."

"Everyone knows cats are good at serenading," said the donkey. "Come with us to Bremen. I am sure you can become a musician there."

The cat agreed. She hopped onto the dog's back, and she joined her companions in practicing their music. The donkey said, "Hee, haw! Hee, hee, haw!" The dog barked, "Bow, woof, bow, wow!" The cat sang a melodious "Mew, mew, meoooOOW!"

After traveling some distance, the three animals came to a farmyard. On the gate a woebegone rooster perched, his head hanging low.

"What makes you so sad?" asked the donkey.

"I am getting too old to greet the dawn," replied the rooster, "but I still have plenty of singing left in me. I heard you singing on your way, and I wanted to join in."

"Well," said the donkey, "we are going to Bremen to become musicians. Since you have such a fine loud voice, why don't you come with us?"

The rooster agreed. He hopped up onto the cat's head. Then they all practiced in harmony. The donkey sang, "Hee, haw! Hee, hee, haw!" The dog barked, "Bow, woof, bow, wow!" The cat sang a melodious "Mew, mew, meoooOOW!" And the rooster crowed magnificently, "Cock-a-doodle-de-doo!"

They could not reach Bremen that day, so they decided to spend the night in the woods.

The donkey and the dog lay down under a large tree. The cat nestled in the branches, and the rooster flew up to the very top.

Before they fell asleep, the rooster saw a light in the distance. "There must be a house over there," he said.

"Let us go and look," said the donkey. "There may be shelter and food for us." The dog hopped onto the donkey's back, the cat climbed onto the dog's back, and the rooster clambered up to stand on the donkey's head.

12

The donkey walked toward the light, carrying his friends. The light was coming from a lamp inside a cozy little cottage. The donkey stopped at the window. They all looked in.

They saw a table laid out with plenty to eat, and a group of raccoons enjoying themselves. There were sacks of stolen grain lying all around the room.

"Robbers, by the look of them," said the hound.

"I wish we could get inside," said the donkey. "It looks warm and cozy."

"And just look at that vegetable stew!" exclaimed the cat.

"Yum!" said the rooster.

The dog drooled. "I am very hungry!"

13

"Maybe they would give us some supper if they liked our singing," said the donkey. He stood up against the windowsill, and the companions all began to perform their music. The donkey sang, "Hee, haw! Hee, hee, haw!" The dog barked, "Bow, woof, bow, wow!" The cat sang a melodious "Mew, mew, meoooOOW!" And the rooster crowed magnificently, "Cock-a-doodle-de-doo!" The window rattled with the sound.

The robbers fled in terror.

"They must have liked our music," said the donkey. "See all the good food they left us."

The musicians went inside and ate their fill of the robbers' feast.

When the four musicians had finished eating, each found a comfortable sleeping place for himself. The donkey lay down on the floor, the dog crouched behind the door, the cat curled up on the hearth, and the rooster perched under the eaves. Soon they fell asleep.

The robbers were watching the house from a distance. Now they were getting soaked by rain.

"We should not have run away," said one robber. "I will go back and see if it is safe."

The robber went into the cottage. In the darkness the cat's fiery eyes looked like burning coals. When the robber came close, the cat leapt up and hissed at him.

As the robber rushed for the door the dog sprang up and barked at him.

The robber bumped into the donkey, who brayed and stamped. All the while the rooster cried, "Cock-a-doodle-de-doo," with all his might.

The terrified robber ran back to his companions as fast as his legs would carry him.

"There are wild things in that house," he told them. "One flew at me and hissed. Then one by the door growled. A monster screamed and pounded the earth. And up above sat a ghost who cried, 'Catch the scoundrel, do!'"

The robbers ran away and never came back.

It so happened that the cottage belonged to a farmer who had long wished to chase away the robbers who stole from him. When he came by in the morning to scare the robbers, he heard the musicians singing. He peered through the window and saw the four friends sitting around the table and enjoying their music. The donkey sang, "Hee, haw! Hee, hee, haw!" The dog barked, "Bow, woof, bow, wow!" The cat sang a melodious "Mew, mew, meoooOOW!" And the rooster crowed magnificently, "Cock-a-doodle-de-doo!"

"That sound will keep the robbers away," the farmer called through the window. "Stay here as long as you like. I'm getting too old to chase robbers."

The four musicians liked their new home. And there they remain, making music to their hearts' content.

The Elves and the Shoemaker

Once upon a time there was a kind shoemaker. Though he worked very hard, he grew so poor that at last he had only enough leather left for one pair of shoes.

One winter night he cut out the shoes, but he was too tired to finish them. He left the leather on his workbench and decided to make the shoes the next morning.

The shoemaker didn't know what he and his wife would do now that all the leather was used up, for he had no money to buy more. But despite their troubles, the shoemaker and his wife slept soundly that night.

Early the next morning the shoemaker woke up. He got dressed and went into the shop to make his last pair of shoes.

18

He picked up a hammer and sat down at the bench. What was this?!! The shoemaker thought he must be dreaming! He blinked his eyes, but it was no dream! On the very spot where he had left the leather the night before, there was a finished pair of beautiful shoes.

He called his wife into the shop and showed her the shoes. "They're splendid!" she exclaimed. "When did you make them?"

"I didn't make them," the shoemaker replied. "I just found them here!"

The shoemaker put the shoes in the window, hoping that someone would buy them. Soon the door swung open and a fine gentleman walked into the shop.

"I must have those wonderful shoes," he said. "I've never seen any like them. The stitches are so small and delicate!"

The shoemaker sold the shoes to the gentleman, who paid a very high price for them.

With the money the shoemaker was able to buy enough leather for two more pairs of shoes. And he had enough left over to buy a soup bone for dinner.

That night he cut out the leather. But he was very hungry, and he could smell the soup his wife was cooking. "I'll make the shoes tomorrow," he said, and he went to eat dinner.

The next morning he found two pairs of elegant shoes on his workbench. He showed them to his wife. "Who can be making these marvelous shoes?" she said.

The shoemaker wondered, too. Once again he placed the shoes in the window, and again he didn't have long to wait before the door swung open. This time there were two customers, and they both paid the shoemaker handsomely.

Now the shoemaker had enough money to buy leather for four pairs of shoes.

Things went on this way for some time. Every night the shoemaker cut the leather and went to sleep. And every morning he found more beautiful shoes on his workbench!

The shoemaker was growing rich.

One evening the shoemaker said to his wife, "It's nearly Christmas, and we still don't know who is making the shoes. We cannot go another day without finding out who is helping us."

So together the shoemaker and his wife thought of a plan. Instead of going to sleep that night, they hid in the shop.

At midnight two tiny elves came into the room. The shoemaker and his wife watched in amazement as the elves stitched and sewed and hammered.

Soon the bench was filled with shiny new shoes. The moment their work was finished the elves vanished.

"How wondrous!" the shoemaker cried. "We must do something for those tiny creatures who have been so kind."

"Well," said his wife, "the poor little things had no clothes or shoes on, and they must get very cold at this time of year."

So the shoemaker and his wife made two tiny suits of clothing for the elves.

The next night they laid the things they had made on the table and once again hid behind the curtain.

Just at midnight the elves came into the room. When they saw the clothes, they were overjoyed. They tried them on and found that they fitted just right.

The elves danced around the room and sang a merry song.

At last the elves danced out the door, never to return.

But the shoemaker and his wife, who had paid back kindness with kindness, never wanted for anything, and they lived happily for a good long time.

The Emperor's New Clothes

Many years ago there lived an emperor who was very fond of new clothes. One day two impostors, pretending to be weavers, came to the city where he lived. It was said that the color and design of their cloth was beautiful and that the fabric possessed a magical quality of being invisible to anyone who was stupid.

"I would like to have clothes made of that material," the emperor thought. "Then I could tell the clever from the stupid in my kingdom." He ordered a suit from the two impostors, and he gave them a large sum of money.

The impostors began their work. They set up their looms and asked for the finest silk and the most beautiful gold thread to work into their cloth. They put the fine things into their pockets and pretended to work at the bare looms till late at night.

"I should like to know how the weavers are getting on with the cloth," the emperor thought after a few days. "I will send my wise old prime minister to the weavers. He will be able to see if the fabric is all they promised it to be."

So the old prime minister went to the room where the two impostors were working at their bare looms. "Goodness gracious!" the prime minister thought. He opened his eyes wide, but he could not see anything.

Both impostors asked whether he did not think the design pretty and the colors beautiful. The poor old prime minister opened his eyes still wider. "Can it be possible," he thought, "that I am stupid? No one must find out!"

"It is very pretty! Quite beautiful!" the old minister said aloud, looking through his spectacles. "I shall tell the emperor."

The weavers pointed out all the different colors and explained the unusual design. The old minister paid great attention and used the very same words to describe the wonderful cloth to the emperor.

The impostors now asked for more money, more silk, and more gold thread, which they kept for themselves. Not a single thread was put upon the looms, though the impostors continued to pretend they were working.

Soon the emperor sent the grand duke to see the weavers and find out when the cloth would be ready. The grand duke looked and looked, but he could see nothing on the bare loom.

"Well, isn't that beautiful cloth?" the two impostors asked when they had explained the magnificent design.

"If I am stupid," the grand duke thought, "I must never let anyone find out." So he praised the fabric, which he did not see. "Oh, it is lovely," he said when he described it to the emperor.

Everyone in the city was talking of the magnificent fabric.

Now the emperor wanted to see it for himself. With all his courtiers he went to the two impostors. He found them busily working, though he couldn't see a thread.

"Isn't it magnificent?" the two impostors asked. "Your Majesty should look closely and examine the design and beautiful colors."

"My word!" the emperor thought. "Why, I see nothing at all. Am I stupid? It would be terrible for anyone to find out."

"Yes, it is very beautiful!" he said aloud. "I approve!"

All the courtiers looked and looked, and they saw no more than the emperor. But they didn't wish to be thought stupid, so they advised the emperor to wear clothes of that magnificent fabric in a grand procession. The emperor awarded medals to both the impostors, and he dubbed them court weavers.

The impostors were up the whole night before the procession was to take place. Everyone could see that they were very busy. They pretended they were taking the cloth off the loom. They sewed with needles without thread. At last they said, "Now the clothes are ready."

The emperor came to see his new suit. Both impostors raised their arms exactly as if they were holding things up. They said, "These are the trousers, this is the coat, here is the cloak. The cloth is so light that you might think you have nothing on. If Your Imperial Majesty will please take off your clothes, we will put the new clothes on you before the mirror."

The emperor took off his clothes, and the impostors pretended to help him on with the new garments. The emperor turned about before the mirror.

"Oh, how beautifully they fit!" he said. "The pattern and colors are perfect. This is a magnificent outfit!"

A servant came in and said, "The procession is waiting outside, Your Majesty."

"Well, I am ready," the emperor said.

The pages stooped and pretended to pick up the end of the emperor's cloak, which they then pretended to hold, for they would not have it appear that they could not see anything.

So the emperor walked in the procession, under a magnificent canopy.

All the people in the street and in the windows said, "The emperor's clothes are not to be equaled." No one would say that he did not see anything, for he would have been thought stupid.

But one little child had heard nothing about the emperor's new clothes. "He has nothing on," the child said when the emperor passed.

Some people laughed at the child and whispered the joke to one another. Then everyone looked again at the emperor.

"He has nothing on!" all the people cried at last.

It appeared to the emperor that they were right. But he said to himself, "Well, anyway, I must go on with the procession." And he kept walking till he got home and put on clothes that he could see!

Stone Soup

One day, in a small town in a lonely part of the country, a child saw three wayfarers coming down the road. "Strangers are coming to town!" he cried, running through the streets.

Now, the townspeople had just harvested their crops, and they were storing away food for the winter.

"Strangers coming here?" said one. "They'll have come a long way, and they're bound to be hungry!"

"After all our hard work, they'll want us to give them our food!" said another.

"Let's hurry and hide it," said a third. "Then we can tell them we have none to share."

Throughout the town the people hid their food down in cellars, up in attics, under floors, behind doors. Then they shut themselves in their houses and lowered their curtains, so it would appear to the strangers that they did not wish to be bothered.

31

The three wayfarers were only poor fellows trying to make their way in the world. When they reached the town, they were hungry and tired.

"I would like a cup of hot soup," said one.

"Me, too," said the second.

"Let's ask some of the good people of this town if they will give us some," said the third.

So the three friends went to a house and knocked long and hard. After a while, the door opened a crack.

"We are three weary wanderers," said the first friend. "Can you spare a cup of soup for us?"

"No soup here," said a voice inside the house. "There's no food at all in this town. You'd best be on your way." And the door was slammed shut.

The wayfarers tried at other houses with no better luck. At last one of them had an idea.

"The fields and gardens in this town have been picked clean," he said. "There's food here, if only we can get some. We'll have to make stone soup.

"We'll need to gather some things. You start at that house and ask to borrow a kettle," he told one friend. "You start at the neighbor's and ask for kindling wood," he told the other. "I will gather three good round stones."

At the first house the wayfarer said, "Since you haven't any food, may we borrow a kettle for our stone soup?"

"Stone soup? How do you make it?" asked the townsman.

"Lend us your kettle and you will see," said the wayfarer. "We'll give you a taste when it's done."

"Is stone soup good?" asked the townsman.

"Nothing is as good when it's done," said the wayfarer.

He got the kettle, and his friend got the kindling after telling the neighbor about stone soup. Then they set about getting matches and buckets of water, mentioning stone soup at each and every house.

By the time they were back in the square with the things
they had gathered, everyone in town was curious about stone
soup. The townspeople watched from behind their curtains to
see what the wayfarers would do.

They filled the kettle with water. They built a fire and set
the kettle over it. When the water was boiling, they carefully
rolled the three round stones into the pot. Then they sat down,
as if waiting for the soup to cook.

"That's no way to make soup," said a townsman. "That
stone soup needs some carrots. And, well—I guess I can spare
the carrots myself." He ran down to the cellar, took a big bunch
of carrots, and brought them out to the wayfarers in the square.

34

"Well, it's true," said one wayfarer. "Nothing's as good as stone soup with carrots. Thank you." He cut them up and dropped them into the pot.

"Carrots indeed!" said a townswoman who was watching from her house. "That soup needs onions." She took a big bag of onions from under her floor and dragged it into the square.

"Ah, nothing's as good as stone soup with onions," said a wayfarer, starting to peel them. "Thank you."

And so it went. Beets and parsnips, celery and potatoes, barley and peas, were added to the stone soup. Everyone in town brought something tasty for the pot. The wayfarers kept stirring, and soon the odor of delicious soup filled the air.

And when everyone had a taste, they all agreed—nothing's as good as stone soup.

The Sleeping Beauty

In a land far away there lived a king and a queen who said every day, "If only we had a child!" But they had none.

At last the queen had a little girl who was so beautiful that the king could not contain himself for joy, and he prepared a great feast. He invited his relatives, friends, and acquaintances, and also the fairies, hoping that they might bless his child. Seven of them were invited, and the king had seven golden plates made for them to eat from.

There was an eighth fairy in the land, but she was very old, and as no one had seen her for a long time, she had been forgotten. She appeared at the feast, but there was no golden plate for her. One fairy, seeing the old one's anger at this, hid behind a curtain to watch what would happen.

36

When the feast came to an end, the fairies were each to present the child with a magic gift. The first gave her beauty. The second gave her wisdom. The third gave her sweetness. The fourth, a charming voice to sing with. The fifth, grace to dance with. The sixth fairy gave her the gift of skill to work with.

The old fairy then stood up and called out in a loud voice, "Here is my gift: In her fifteenth year the princess shall prick herself on a spindle and fall lifeless to the floor." And without another word, she turned and left the hall.

Everyone was terror-stricken, but the seventh fairy, whose wish was still unspoken, stepped from behind the curtain. She could not cancel the curse, but she could soften it. She said, "It shall be just a deep sleep lasting but one hundred years."

The king was anxious to guard his dear child from this misfortune. He commanded that all the spindles in the whole kingdom be burned.

As time went on, all the promises of the fairies came true. The princess grew up so beautiful, wise, sweet, and clever that everyone who saw her could not but love her.

It happened that on the very day when she was fifteen years old, the king and queen were away from home and the princess was left quite alone in the castle. She wandered about, and at last she came to an old tower. She went up a winding staircase and reached a little door. She pushed it open. She found a little room where an old woman sat with a spindle.

"Good day," said the princess. "What are you doing?"

"I am spinning," said the old woman.

"What is the thing that whirls around?" asked the princess. She reached for the spindle and pricked her finger.

She dropped onto a nearby bed and fell asleep. This same deep sleep spread over the castle.

When the king and queen came home and stepped into the hall, they fell asleep. All of the servants slept, too. Ladybugs and bumblebees on a vine in the courtyard fell asleep, as did the butterflies on the roof and the flies on the wall.

Around the castle a thick hedge of briar roses began to grow. Every year, for one hundred years, it grew higher and thicker, until at last it covered the whole castle. The people living nearby told the story of the lovely sleeping Briar Rose, as the king's daughter was now called.

After a hundred years, a prince came to the country and heard an old man tell of the castle that stood behind the briar hedge, in which a beauty called Briar Rose was asleep.

The young prince said, "I wish to go and look upon the lovely Briar Rose."

Now, this was the day when Briar Rose was to wake up again. When the prince approached the briar hedge, its thickly entwined branches parted, making way for him to enter.

In the courtyard he saw ladybugs and bumblebees sleeping on a honeysuckle vine. Butterflies, lost in their dreams, were perched on the roof. When he went into the castle, the flies were asleep on the wall. By the throne lay the king and queen.

At last he reached the tower and opened the door into the little room where Briar Rose was asleep. There she lay, looking so beautiful that he could not take his eyes off her. He bent down and gave her a kiss.

As he touched her, Briar Rose opened her eyes and looked lovingly at him. Then they went down from the tower together, and the king, the queen, and all the courtiers woke up and looked at each other with astonished eyes. The ladybugs began moving about, and the bumblebees crept in and out of the sweet honeysuckle blossoms. The butterflies on the roof fluttered and flew away. The flies on the wall began to buzz.

The prince and the princess Briar Rose were soon married.

The wedding was celebrated with much splendor, and they lived happily ever after.

The Princess and the Pea

There was once a prince who wished to marry a real princess, and so he traveled around the world to find one. He met many young women who claimed to be princesses, but he could not be certain that this was true. Very sadly he returned to the palace alone.

Then, on a terrible stormy night, when the roar of thunder shook the walls and rain spilled from the sky like a waterfall, the palace gate-bell clanged. The old king went to see who was there. The queen and the prince stood by. They saw a beautiful princess, but what a state she was in! The rain soaked her clothing and her crown was dripping. The king beckoned her to come inside.

"Who are you?" he then asked.

"A princess," said the princess.

"A real princess?" asked the prince.

"Why, yes, of course," said the princess.

"Well, that we'll soon find out," the old queen thought. She went into the bedroom where the princess was to sleep that night. She took all the things off the bed. Then she placed a small pea on the bed and put the mattress on top of it.

Then the queen cried out, "More mattresses!"

Chambermaids struggled in with all the spare mattresses they could find. They piled them on the bed.

"Still not enough!" said the queen. "Bring every mattress in the castle!"

In came the cook, moaning and groaning and dragging her mattress. It was as purple as fine grapes. Her daughter came next, with a mattress as blue as the summer sky. Then came the two castle guards, balancing their mattresses on top of their helmets. One mattress was as green as young grass, and the other was as yellow as rich butter. Three musicians brought theirs—one orange, like ripe pumpkins, the other as pink as a newborn babe. The last was bright red, like the flowers that grew in rows around the palace.

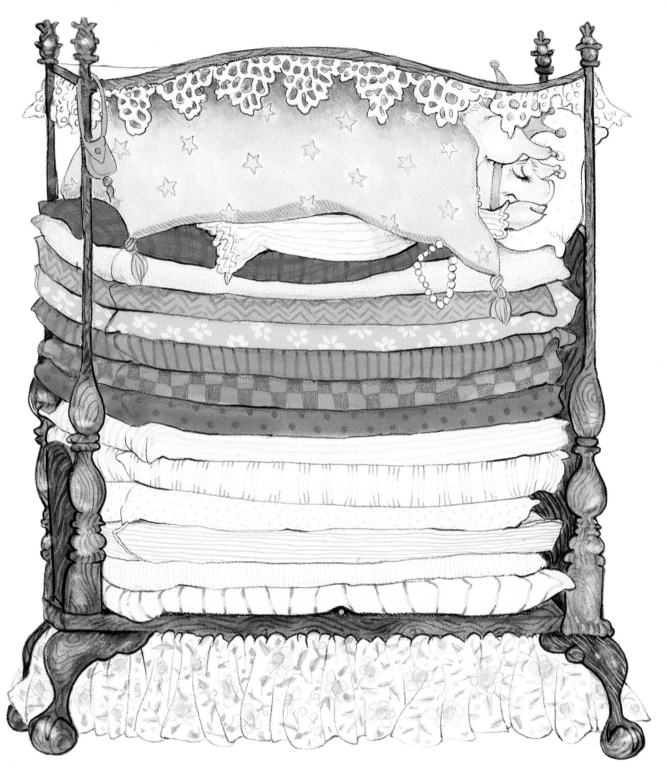

"That will do," said the queen at last. "Summon the princess. It is time for bed."

The princess arrived and exclaimed, "Why, it's a rainbow bed! What a fitting treat for a princess. Thank you!"

She needed a ladder to climb onto the bed, but she was soon settled under a fine feather quilt. It was covered with pale blue silk, embroidered with stars.

Then everyone went to bed—not too happily without their mattresses—and the lights were turned out.

In the morning the queen came into the room and asked the princess how she had slept.

"Oh, badly!" the princess answered. "I scarcely closed my eyes the whole night. Something hard was in the bed, and I couldn't stop tossing and turning."

The queen called for the prince. "This is a real princess," she declared. "She felt a pea through thirteen mattresses. Only a real princess is able to feel that!"

So the prince married the princess, and the pea was placed in the royal museum, where it may still be seen.

Now good night!